I Love Saturday

I Love Saturday

BY PATRICIA REILLY GIFF

Illustrated by Frank Remkiewicz

VIKING KESTREL

VIKING KESTREL
Published by the Penguin Group
Viking Penguin, a division of Penguin Books USA Inc.,
40 West 23rd Street, New York, New York 10010, U.S.A.
Penguin Books Ltd, 27 Wrights Lane, London W8 5TZ, England
Penguin Books Australia Ltd, Ringwood, Victoria, Australia
Penguin Books Canada Ltd, 2801 John Street, Markham, Ontario, Canada L3R 1B4
Penguin Books (N.Z.) Ltd, 182–190 Wairau Road, Auckland 10, New Zealand

Penguin Books Ltd, Registered Offices: Harmondsworth, Middlesex, England

First published in 1989 by Viking Penguin, a division of Penguin Books USA Inc.
10 9 8 7 6 5 4 3 2 1
Text copyright © Patricia Reilly Giff, 1989
Illustrations copyright © Frank Remkiewicz, 1989
All rights reserved

Library of Congress Cataloging-in-Publication Data
Giff, Patricia Reilly.   I love Saturday /
   Patricia Reilly Giff ; pictures by Frank Remkiewicz.   p.   cm.
      Summary: On Saturday morning Katie, who lives in Greenwich
   Village, plays checkers, helps paint the hallway, receives a sugar
   cookie from Mrs. Zelinsky, and keeps a secret.
      ISBN 0-670-81409-1
      [1. Greenwich Village (New York, N.Y.)—Fiction.   2. Secrets—
   Fiction.]   I. Remkiewicz, Frank, ill.   II. Title.
   PZ7.G3626Ia1   1989   [E]—dc20   89-8984

Printed in Japan.
Set in Century Schoolbook.

For my son Bill, with love

P.R.G.

For Sarah, Jessica, and Madaleine,
who also love Saturdays

F.R.

Saturday used to be my best day.
But now there's something different.
It's all because of Jessica Jeanne, the TV queen.
I'll tell you all about it.

First about me. My name is Katie Cobb.
K for Katie. *C* for Cobb.
I used to do it backwards.
But that was a long time ago, last year.

I have one thing, a secret.
Nobody knows about it except Charles and Dexter,
my mother and father, and my red cat Willie, of course.
Maybe I'll tell about it later.

I live in the neatest place.
It's called Greenwich Village.
It has tall, gray buildings, and brown houses
with stairs that go up to the second floor,
and a dance studio where ballerinas practice.
Car horns go *blaaaaaah*, and people bump umbrellas
into each other, and have to say "excuse me,"
twenty times in a block.
But I don't want to talk about that right now.
I want to talk about Saturday.

On Saturdays I wake up early.
I play a game of checkers by myself,
and then a game of jacks.
After a while I get tired of always winning so . . .
I put on my skinny jeans
and my shirt that says: QUIET PLEASE.
I tuck a tiny piece of blanket into my pocket.
(That's part of the secret.)

Then I zip down to 3B to see if Mrs. Zelinsky
is up yet.
She has the best sugar cookies in the world.
Even Charles the doorman says so.
"It's too early, Katie," Mrs. Zelinsky always says.
But she hands me a sugar cookie anyway. . .

which I eat around the edges
as I zoom up to the fourth floor.
Dexter, the handyman, is painting the walls,
except that he's off on Saturdays.
He always leaves the can of green
and a huge fat brush in the corner.
So I paint a tall *K* for Katie and a *C* for Cobb.
Mr. Curso pops his head out of 4F.
"It's a good thing Dexter says you're his helper,"
he says. "Otherwise you'd be in trouble."

I help Charles stack the mail, dust the lady
on the table, and neaten up the desk.

Charles says, "I'd never get finished
without you, Katie."
I nod my head, "I know."

Then I race down Sixth Avenue to the market where
John tips his straw hat at me, and wipes his hands
on his long white apron.
He gives me a bologna end, and a slice of liverwurst
for the trip back.
"How's my favorite girl?" he always asks.

But this Saturday, *this Saturday*,
something terrible happened.
Mrs. Zelinsky in 3B didn't even open her door.
"I gave out my last cookie," she said.

And on the fourth floor, someone had painted already.
The brush was a mess and so was the floor . . .
with dots all over the rug.
And on the wall was a big green

And what else was:
The mail was sorted,

and the table with the lady was dusted,
and the desk was neat as a pin.

At the market, John had no bologna ends,
and only half a slice of liverwurst was left.

I bumped my umbrella down the street,
and came inside again.
There was Willie, *my* red cat, sitting on the lap
of a girl with a round face, a squished-in nose,
long skinny legs with dots of green paint,
and a red beaded pocketbook with a silver string.
(She had sugar cookie crumbs all over her mouth.)

No fair.

I put my hands on my hips.
"How come you're doing all my stuff?"

"I'm visiting my grandmother,
Mrs. Zelinsky."

"Come on, Willie," I said.
"Let's go upstairs."

"My name is Jessica Jeanne," she said.
"I love elevators, sugar cookies,
and bologna ends,
and sometimes I paint."

    "Come on, Willie. Let's go."

"I love to watch television.
My father calls me
Jessica Jeanne the TV queen."

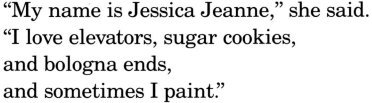

    "Come on, Willie."

"I have a checkers game,
and Parchesi,
and Don't Break the Ice . . .
a jump rope with red plaid string . . .

    "I mean it, Willie."

I have fourteen books on my shelf,
and you know what?"

In the elevator,
I pressed the button for 5,
and Jessica Jeanne pressed 3,
while Willie stood in the middle.

"It's no fun to play alone,"
said Jessica Jeanne.
She leaned over.
"What's in your pocket?"

                                        "It's a secret."

"I have a blanket, too."

                                        "You do?"

"But I'm going to stop
sucking my thumb next Sunday."

                                        "Me, too."

On Saturday I take the elevator from 5
to Jessica Jeanne at 3.
First we get a sugar cookie from Mrs. Zelinsky,
then on 4 we paint the wall.

Downstairs we help Charles
stack the mail,
dust the lady,
neaten up the desk.

We bump umbrellas down the street
for bologna ends
and liverwurst
at the market.

Saturday is the best day
for Jessica Jeanne and me.
And Willie, my red cat,
of course.